Paddy Dies

Stewart Parker

SUMMER PALACE PRESS

First published in 2004 by

Summer Palace Press
Cladnageeragh, Kilbeg, Kilcar, County Donegal, Ireland

Printed by Nicholson & Bass Ltd.

A catalogue record for this book is available
from the British Library

ISBN   0   9544752   5   9

This book is printed on elemental chlorine-free paper

Stewart Parker, playwright, novelist and poet, was born on 20th October, 1941 in Belfast. He was educated at Strand Primary School, Ashfield Boys' School and Sullivan Upper School. From 1959 until 1964 he studied English Literature at Queen's University, Belfast, first with Professor Butter and then with myself. He gained a BA in English Literature in 1963 and an MA in 1966. His studies at Queen's University were impeded by the onset of cancer and he spent most of a year in hospital, during which he suffered the amputation of his left leg.

He early on gained a local reputation as a poet and was a key figure in the Belfast Group, a creative writing workshop whose notable members in the early 1960s included Seamus Heaney and James Simmons, and later Michael Longley. His poems, 'Crutch' and 'Coming Out' appeared in *Young Commonwealth Poets '65*, edited by P.L. Brent (London: Heinemann, 1965). 'Paddy Dies' and 'Health' appeared in *British Poetry since 1945*, edited by Edward Lucie-Smith (Harmondsworth, Penguin Books, 1970). A long poem, 'The Casualty's Meditation' was published in 1966 as a pamphlet in a much sought-after series, Belfast Festival Publications.

His main interest, however, was to lie in drama. He married Kate Ireland on 26th August, 1964 and that year they went to Clinton, New York. Here he became an instructor in English and Creative Writing at Hamilton College. Parker moved to Cornell University in 1967 and returned to Belfast in 1969, determined to earn his living as a writer. He involved himself in studying the Irish language. He began a regular pop-music review column in the *Irish Times* and contributed articles on literary and theatrical subjects to that and several other newspapers and journals. His play, *The Iceberg*, was broadcast in 1975 on BBC Radio, and *I'm a Dreamer, Montreal* was broadcast on radio, televised by Thames in 1979 and was awarded the Christopher Ewart-Biggs Memorial Prize. Other plays pioneered on radio included *The Kamikaze Ground Staff Reunion Dinner* (1979) which won the Giles Cooper Award for 1980 and was televised the following year, and *The Traveller* (1985). *Catchpenny Twist* was first staged at the Peacock Theatre, Dublin in 1977 and was adapted the same year for BBC Television in the Play for Today series.

He served for a time as Resident Playwright at the King's Head Theatre, Islington. *Spokesong* had been produced at the Dublin Theatre Festival in 1975 and was revived at the King's Head in 1976. It won the

Evening Standard Most Promising Playwright Award and was transferred to the Vaudeville Theatre in London's West End in February 1977. *Spokesong* also opened at the Long Wharf Theatre in New Haven, Connecticut in 1978, and was brought to the Circle in the Square Theatre on Broadway in 1979. It represented Parker's breakthrough as a writer.

In 1982 Parker moved to London and wrote mainly for television: *Iris in the Traffic, Ruby in the Rain* (1981); *Joyce in June* (1982); *Blue Money* (1984) and *Radio Pictures* (1985). *Northern Star, Heavenly Bodies* and *Pentecost*, published under the collective title *Three Plays for Ireland* (London: Oberon Books, 1989), constituted a major work of Irish drama and marked the summit of Parker's achievement.

Stewart Parker again developed cancer. He died on 2nd November 1988, at the age of 47.

Professor Philip Hobsbaum,
Department of English,
University of Glasgow.

Editors' Notes

Some of these poems were available only in manuscript or typescript. For others, we used the versions which appeared in *The Casualty's Meditation* (Belfast Festival Publications 1966) and *Maw* (Belfast Festival Publications 1968). With regard to the *Ulster Sequence* or *Parker's Fitts*, there is an undated, handwritten list containing twenty-six titles, and we have followed this sequence. As far as we can ascertain, numbers 21, 22, 23, 25 and 26 are missing or were never written. As a general rule, we have used the latest existing version (often the BBC radio script with Stewart's handwritten emendations). Some of the idiosyncrasies of spelling and punctuation seem to have been intentional.

Acknowledgments

We would like to thank Professor Philip Hobsbaum for co-editing the book, for his constancy, help and advice, and for providing the introduction; John Fairleigh, Director of the Stewart Parker Trust; Marilynn Richtarik, Stewart Parker's biographer, for her generous suggestions and use of text; Lynne Parker, for providing family manuscripts and for her support; Lesley Bruce for allowing access to Stewart Parker's papers; Jack Pakenham for permitting the use of his painting on the cover; Special Collections, Queen's University, Belfast, for their enthusiasm and helpfulness; Rosemary Hobsbaum, who liaised when Philip was unavailable; Robbie Meredith, Literature Officer at the Arts Council of Northern Ireland; Nicholson and Bass, in particular Don Hawthorn and David Anderson, for their expertise and co-operation; Paula McFetridge and Mike Blair of the Lyric Theatre for inviting the book to be launched there, and all those people who have agreed to read and provide music.

CONTENTS

Paddy Dies

Paddy dies: you never knew him.
A deaf hunchback in a home for the old.

Deafness drew the blind of his soul.
Nobody knew him. Nobody knew him.

A wild animal in him reared
Up one night, I saw his eyes
And for three days he disappeared
They found him sleeping in a pig-sty.
I wonder if sixty years ago
He slept tender in a girl's breasts?

He seems to sleep hard now.
His bony umbrella collapsed at last.

Coming Out

I had often dreamt of my clothes
On the nights that were merely thick and heavy with
pain . . . . .
Laundered shirt crinkly with goodness,
Black elegance of my tapered shoes,
(The bandages crusted with blood on me,
The tortured pyjamas crawled up my arms),
Chunky sweater, flannels slim as a flame . . . . . .
But when they came
It was evident that they belonged to another man.
They bit at my neck, heightened the stooning rhythm in
my leg's stump.

"Well, it's the Big Day!"
The Sister's cursory handshake,
A few tears from the night-nurse I had snogged in a
weaker moment,
Then it was down the resounding corridor busy as a
trench,
The metal crutches clinking like chain-mail,
My father thoughtful beside me.

Coming through Extern,
The twilight was pregnant with sick bodies.
"It's like the war";
Each separate body waited for its name.
We passed into the world's blare.
My eyes stuttered at the naked day.
"How do you feel?" – "Reborn." I really did
But my other voice cried Liar!
Your leg that inched its way to tall for nineteen years
is dead!
I sprawled into the car. I had come out.

We have to wait while an ambulance
Bullies its way through the main gate,
I watch the pas de deux (with stretcher)
Of the entire familiar dance.
"It never stops, does it?" "The poor bastards."
The journey home begins
Along the streets choking with people
And the bus queues are still queuing and the cars are
still waiting for the unchanging lights.
Only the clocks have changed.
And a massive familiar surgeon is at my elbow,
to welcome me back home into the hospital.

Epithalamion

Spread the white linen, stiff as bread,
the counterpane, patterned with red roses,
spattered with blots of blood;
now the bed's made.

The first pain comes at dawn, dim sky shot with red,
when life rattles in the girl's belly.
Lay out the brave thighs.
Each dragging hour is bled
dry, until, her eyes wild, she sees the white
room shudder with her final strain.
Spread out the counterpane.

The last pain comes at night, the blinds go down,
when the old man fights amidst whispers until,
driven within the gates, he is forced down street
after long street,
turns at bay in his city's heart
and blood explodes across his brain.
He is gone, say the whispers, he is gone.
Lay out the white linen.

In the afternoon stillness, we spread our poor nakedness,
patterned with red roses.
Our bodies stiffen like bread.
Ticaticatica of the watch on my wrist, spasm
of the pulse beneath the watch
join
in the waltz of our hands and our mouths
drown
in our thrusting loins, and when
our love locks in final coitus,
That is defeat for the first pain and the last pain.

Spread the white linen, stiff as bread,
the counterpane, patterned with red roses,
spattered with blots of blood;
now the bed's made.

Railroad Ode

beginning with the entrance of the Burlington Morning Zephyr
august and irrestible as an ocean roller
amongst the fussy dusty commuter trains
her one white eye in the forehead
and the steady clang of her voice
and her airbrakes like the calf muscles
of a prima ballerina, easing her
to a dead
halt.

In the observation car at midnight
it is pitch dark over the prairies.
From time to time, tall as a granary,
a phantasmal face rears up in a drive-in movie,
the farmers' sons of Illinois
huddled in cars at its throat;
or violet lightning photographs
the flat skyline, the immense swathes of cumulus.
Nothing but the distant owl-hoot
of the whistle: until
in the seat behind, a dream-craven old man's deliriums
begin.

On the tracks at Billings Montana
the Burlington #30 for Denver (one coach)
is now boarding. There are eight passengers
and the conductor: the young Indian mother
is reading *True Secrets*, her son is playing cowboys.
All day clacking down the spine of Wyoming
corrals turning to desert
desert turning to sagebrush, mountains
climbing higher and turning blood-red,
night flowing into Wind River Canyon,
and then stumbling sleepily off
dawn rustling around somewhere over Cheyenne.

Here is the song of the porter
on the San Francisco Chief: - Clovis, all change for
Farwell Bovina Friona Black Hereford
Umbarger Canyon Amarillo Panhandle White Deer
Pampa Miami Canadian Higgins Shattuck
Gage Fargo Woodward Mooreland Waynoka
Alva Kiowa Attica Harper Wellington
Wichita Newton Topeka Kansas City Chicago.

concluding with the Southern Pacific Sunset Limited
clattering over the Mississippi
on the run in to New Orleans.
I am pretending that this is the Rock Island Line
and that Poor Paddy, Railroad Bill and Casey Jones
are at my elbow;

and they are.

Derangement in San Francisco I

He squats him down
on the stone steps of the Bank of America
shrivelled and mangy as a cormorant
trapped inland.
The tourists, ravening at the cable-car turntable,
clench in a circle round him
(what's on their minds,
dat coalblack mammy from Alabammy
in de cotton fields back home?)

and round him on the steps
the traffic in dollars
wadded close to the citizens' hearts
flows on unheeding.
Wassy takin from that paper bag, maw?
Get that – it's a pink phone!
The receiver stark as a doll's elbow
Against the raddled ebony cheek;
he dials.

Derangement in San Francisco II

Sheet drawn to the chin,
staring into the writhing darkness,
listening to nightlife.

Across the alley,
the Ladies and Gents cataract, snigger, scrawl,
offer themselves. Next door,
an electronic organ jabs and pummels
the fetid air, to pace the flopping
of two bare breasts at debilitated men
eternally tantalised in the search for a mother.
Ten feet away, behind a door,
a ghetto riots in the skull of a woman
alone and old, sirening upwards like a foetus in agony
so almost-human the scalp crawls:
send the devil send the devil
outta this room lawd lawd

Watch stops dead at a minute to three.
Clammily the night digests me
lodged forever in its maw.

Strip Cartoon

1.
Maw watches Mao

Appearing over the ridge: – Get behind them

Wagons!

2.
Mao watches butch marines

Aping old John

Wayne movies on the newsreels.

3.
Mocked negroes, blazing

Away like mobsters is

What the white marines watch.

4.
Mordantly, the negroes

Are watching the fat cop

Whose belly is Maw.

5.
Me is what the cop is watching: – Goddam hairy

Alien

Weirdo.

6.
Me?…watching

A girl, wishing I knew

What happens after the poem.

The Casualty Meditates upon His Journey

1.
Open or closed, my eyes see
traction: pulleys and joists to support broken limbs
in their white casing; like cranes supporting girders
the city's landscape is littered with cranes,
the poking broken fingers of some vast wreckage,
of some smashed fuselage:
the streets must be teeming with images.

A Friday morning in Summer,
the cranes are being crucified against the morning sky.
Out on the waste ground, the factory chimney staggers
and slowly arcs to the ground beneath the surgeon's saw
mechanical grab claws at the rubble of a Victorian pub
the dentist's pliers wrench at the molar.
the steam roller's hot tar anaesthetises the pavement,
the steel needle slides beneath the skin
pneumatic drills concuss and fracture the concrete a
few shavings are whittled off the femur
oxyacetylene cauterises the iron beam the inspector
unscrews the water main and explodes it on the street
blood or bile
clot the brain and blot the world-view.

Of the war's violence, I remember only
a massive iron ball which swung against the wall of
the air-raid shelter, it shattering like burnt bacon.
The charred fragments were our relics,
the fire burns on.
Out at the city's edge, the oil-refinery's waste
flames at the top of its tower eternally
above the city's rubbish dump
where as a child I wade knee-high in books,
loose leaves ripped from the boards
all pulped to a meaninglessness
like the Auschwitz piles,
slide down the side of the mound
in a minor avalanche to land on cinders shovelled black
this morning from yesterday's fires,
and more books and books explaining books
which the binmen collect and eject doing a job that
nobody wants to but somebody etc;
and poke among the decomposing prams
and beds and flags and wirelesses
and the rest of yesterday's wreckage.

2.

A window must be open.
Down there,
growl of traffic, snicker of discarded newspapers.
A dry wind fans the face and memory:
remember the shop windows on a Saturday evening
in Autumn –
Here, a tall lamp with conical red shade
        the wide bed, grained polished wood and
        ample yellow counterpane
        all on a plush deep scarlet carpet
        and the tall mysterious dressing-table
        with her brushes and combs and small secret
        bottles and the benevolent wardrobe peering over
        ready to hold her crisp linens and rustling
        silks and smooth rayons, all of which she
        peels off and hangs there
        and shimmers over to the dressing-table
        to sit naked and brush down
        her sheen of blonde hair, laughing silently
        at the brush clawing through the falling soft clusters
        At a Price You Can Afford!
Here, prams are piled on prams,
        as they are on the rubbish dump,
        as babies are piled on babies.

Here, girl steps into the floodlit window
       trying to look as if she has stripped models before
       and she has, to be sure, but succeeds in making
       this time look like the first time.
       The eyes of the derelict beside me
       are tortured by indecision:
       will it be plastic teats and the bland crotch
       or the alive body curving within the green dress?
       I plump for you, green girl, for you,
       the solid dream demurely stripping the plastic
       dream.
Here, Never was Comfort Accompanied by such Power!
       prostheses, trusses, various kinds of traction
       new legs, new lungs, an artificial brain.
       An entire synthetic man will soon be ready;
       watch our Main Window for Further Announcements

And walk on down to the bus stop.
The girls return from Mecca
Dancing,
harpies and muses all,
coax me with sly glances
passing in threes and fours
from out the mouth of la Plaza
in fives and sixes
vaunt me with rhythmic breasts through their open
coats in sevens and eights the rustle of wicked nylon
invite me with tight skirts in nines and torrents pouring
from the entrance torture me with parted lips and
swinging hips
gaily streaming along the pavement muses and harpies all
the girls on the way from Mecca Dancing.

3.

The evening grinds on like a tired mangle.
Other images return:
outside the gaunt station, the woman peels off a glove and
does not look at the ticket as she slowly tears it up,
riffing through the pieces, cupped in the bare palm,
with sharp nails, finally
letting the hand drop and the pieces flutter.
Outside the gaudy playhouse,
the young man's eyes are on his girl who laughs silently
as he rips the ticket and the pieces scatter
and fall in the gutter, and on the buses
the discarded tickets litter the floor like meal.
The tickets hardly seem to suffer;
the city is all a clutter with such instant deaths,

in winter. Snow floats quietly past the window,
a plague of cabbage-whites glutting the air with deathly stillness,
and under the Ocean Accident and Guarantee
Corporation Limited
people are dying like incredulous fish.

Night floods the city like morphine.
It is Sunday and in the empty church, the text is given
out: Proverbs, 7:6-23,
Her house is the way to hell
going down to the chambers of death;

while out at the city's edge, the oil refinery's waste
burns on insatiably, flickering garishly over the rubbish dump:
to the traveller poised high in the sky's wide maw
or watching the motorway flee like a black eel
or on the wet deck of an ocean liner,
(wondering, is this darkness womb or grave?),
that tower might seem a beacon marking the city
or even a tall torch to guide him home.
Home to the pitch and yaw of emotions
at the city's crowded orifices,
where the pang of aloneness in the strange country
recedes, in the meeting with familiar eyes,
and familiar hands spreadeagle gratefully across hunched shoulders.

For at the window of my house
I looked through my casement,
in the twilight, in the evening, in the black and dark night:
and asked the sky, which was indifferent,
is this darkness womb or tomb?

The night nurse sat at her tiny desk,
the desk-lamp catching her white fall
spread on the shoulders of her green cloak
framing the ageless serene face, and
silently, night's morphine fades,
into the window swims the ancient moon.
He knows he is benign, and impregnates the city
with his fire, and makes the cranes stand up
to tent the hymen of the sky, and says:
Come let us take our fill of love

until the morning.

Postscript

"The pedestrian's left foot was badly crushed and
later had to be amputated."

I am aghast at the man in his sixties
Right leg thin, pink, fleshy and freckled
Left leg tapering to a point at his ankle.

The purple wound strapped into a brown metal foot
He stands between parallel hand-rails holding on
And faces the mirror eleven steps away.

With a violent lurch he starts his journey
Purposive as a fish in a round bowl
Staggering brutally towards himself.

The Broken Lives

I learn the broken lives.
They have cooled on the flat page, I can quote the
relevant lines.

I learn Walt Whitman was a queer, it shows,
His brother Jesse speared by syphilis, wracked in the
relevant asylum, I can
Quote their illiterate mother's relevant letter

oh walt aint it sad…
I learn the broken lives.

Squat skull of Jonathan Swift
Sockets the fattening fattening egg that was his eye,
I can quote Byron's clump clump that shows,
Hopkins stormed by terror in the Dublin darkness,
When the I should have had her when I was in health
of John Keats that shows
in the relevant Italian bed I can quote screams out
My heart goes dead;
I learn the broken lives.

My heart goes dead.
What were they for, the broken lives?
The shuffled relevant pages,
The candidate's critical quote that shows,
The broken lies?

My body ribbons down from my broken mind.
I am shocked by the stark fact of my chest held firm
between the whites of my arms,
Of the living hair that fountains from my brute skull
See, my live is abreath: I sprang to a solid from the
living seed.
I learn the field of broken bullrushes.

I love the broken lives.
They learnt to break.
My heart goes dead with awe
At the terrible win of men who did not girn.
I quote the relevant lives;
They spring from the living page to learn me bend my
spine to the already-begun breaking.
The only whole lives are the broken lives.

Health

Is this God's joke?   my father screamed,
Gripped by the fingers that sprouted and waggled
From the raw holes in my shoulders.
Why blame a God you can't believe in?
Is this the sin of a generation,
The work of hands that worked together
To annihilate hands?   my mother cried.
But I blame no God or man or nation
For my grim disarmament.
Health is my ambition.

Each day, the tin arms swivel.
I tame them, I labour hard for grace, like a
good guitarist, when they swing and glide.
I am satisfied when I lift a cup to my face,
    or write my name.
What I fight is pride
In these small, humble conquests.
Who would be proud of a body?
There is only the daily struggle for peace, and
    the search from day to day for shared
living, for
Life is abundant; life will not be squashed.
There is only the lifting of hands to shake hands
And the lifting of arms to embrace.

Belen, New Mexico

Dusky lady, ancient lady, Houston lady,
lady of the Santa Fe Chief:

Tell me of your sister in San Diego,
show me the plastic billfolds for your grandchildren
that you bought on a day trip to Tijuana.

You say, We're in <u>Ber</u>-lin, fat lady of smiles,
we eat fruit, you're off again in Clovis
to buy cotton cloths with fuzzy Greetings.

The air's full of the delicate pulse
of Summertime, fluting away on the Mexican
lap of the snug boy behind us.

In the dusk, lady, coasting out of scrubby
New Mexico, Houston-bound, eternal lady,

mother of black maws.

Chicago Allegory

Beef Sandwich in Randy's on Michigan Ave
in the Loop. Fat cop pauses on sidewalk
to read the bill of fare. His belly
is the map of America. Folds of fat
bulge on the west and east coasts,
a gun rides the pacific, and
a ready nightstick wags at Europe.

Flick a used scrap of dill pickle
off the formica, swill the rye bread with milk,
tongue out the shreds of beef from crevices.
The black belt scarcely buckles, maw.

Forsyth, North Dakota

Two Indians reeling around on the sidewalk
outside the Howdy Hotel, to open the door
of their battered finny oldsmobile.

From the Vista-Dome of the
Northern Pacific North Coast Limited
distinguished silverhair zooms in on them

with his Bell & Howell. Bluerinse
holds his elbow. A white F carved in the hillside
with a white cross over it.

Aubade

The first of the morning is when a tumbler of ice-water
Slips in my head. I am aware of thirst.

Somehow a boiled cabbage leaf, left in the leaves
Of an old library book, has been stuffed into my jaw.

I chomp feebly on it, finding my chin
Swathed in broken glass. What was that bump

And why are seven pigs being stuck in the windpipe
In my right ear? Ah, they're saying bye-bye.

You mean the raid's over and I should come out now,
Doctor? You mean you removed my spleen?

Clearly I've been tortured, as my neck is broken
And my left arm tied uselessly around it, nearly
Throttling me, like a length of hose.

Never mind. If I lie quiet, I'll die
Soon. And so I comfily do until
The second of the morning which is: my sly
Neighbour tucks a hand grenade under the pillow.
An anaesthetist has no sooner got me still
Again, when a dog barks splinters into
My nerves. And that does it: now I know.

In a flash, I rip off the grubby elastoplasts
From my eyes, and am face to face at last
With the tut-tutting watch and with the morning.

("Why waste a third of your life sleeping!"
But then, why waste <u>two</u>-thirds of it keeping
Awake? I'm exempting, of course, the purists –
Nazis, vegetarians, insomniacs, tourists
All enjoy waking up. And there are morning activities,
Like getting married, taking examinations,
Going to the dentist's, attending funerals,
And kicking old ladies.)

Now it is the third of the morning:
I am sitting on the edge of the bed singing
As I put my shirt on; I am improvising
An atonal air, and the lyrics are going:
<u>Rumpus bleed ag ark too-lay-ing</u>.
I'm wondering if the water that's firing
From my eyes means that I'm actually weeping
And if there's a stethoscope causing the thudding
In my ears, and now I appear to be walking
Into the door-jamb on my way to the bathroom.

Hot water laves my face, sending a thrill
Of sleep through me. I slump against the wall
And fall at once into a paralysed doze.
Staring through crippled eyes at the dozing ghost
In the mirror; and, like the condensation, slide
Slowly down, until I crack my head
On the waste pipe. No sooner have I denied
That it happened than I remember: <u>shaving</u>. The ghost
Peers out from dark green pits and quickly grows
A white, frothy beard. Just look at all
The red trickles appearing! And now I spill
The after-shave, then use it, and drop dead.

(There are people who smoke in the morning!
And people who hold conversations!
Don't they have tear ducts? Do they have friends?)

Now I am driving a car through
The next of the morning, which is sticky with dew.

A bird of some kind is sounding ecstatic.
I think: Beautiful. Beautiful. It's all very balletic,

Gauzes ascending into the vast blue flies
To reveal a tableau of the poised and lithe

Young bodies of trees. The air is tender.
As I park. I dinge a colleague's fender.

And so, like a patient etherised and bloody,
I enter the fug of the classroom
Where my smug students, who believe in eight o'clock classes
Wait sternly to learn from me.
Is my fly unzipped, am I even wearing my trousers?

After a while, I begin falling awake;
Over their heads I can see approaching the dawn
Of the last of the morning.

A Few Notes on New York City

I stood outside a hotel on West 56th. Street and Fifth Avenue.
A girl came through the swing-doors
in the obligatory outfit of the New York whore –
green skin-tight jeans, black leather knee-boots
huge dark glasses; and an inexplicable ancient hag
tagged on behind, fat, Jewish. One glance told the girl
all there was to be known about me –
"Hiya kid, howdya like New York?" she sang in sinus tones
and swept on down towards Broadway, matron waddling in train.

(It is the city of dreadful night and nightmare spires,
and does not consider you worth soliciting if you lack dollars
and can tell at a glance if you don't or do:
but even so, despite its aristocracy,
it will speak to you as it passes: wittily, harshly.)

"There's a big activity in Sherry's bar on Fridays"
said the cab-driver who had agreed to break the law
and take all five of us – for double the fare.
He was being unnecessarily restrictive: the whole city
is a big activity at all its times and in all its places.
Even the citizens get lost in the activity. Another cab-driver
got lost in the endless tangle of Greenwich Village.
At the corner of every block he poked out his head and shouted:
"Hey buddy, where's MacDougal Street?"
It was three in the morning and raining and the streets were still
thronging with excited people like an endless revolution.
It was a parade of strange images –
two men playing chess in a café window, an open fire
in another café window with a bald man with a black beard
cooking something over it, a negro girl in pink jeans
with a white poodle, a glimpse of a bridge, its three huge swoops
across the Hudson traced by white lights.

The images of the daytime are no less strange. In the tiny windows of Tiffany's,
the legendary diamonds, rubies, pearls, are made up to look like
stage-props for a melodrama, or home-made sweets.
The Guggenheim is the embodiment of Dante's inferno;
look down from the top, and you see a massive gyre of light
along which are moving excited human forms, an endless stream
of worshippers spiralling down in their odd pilgrimage.
We saw the Alexander Calder exhibition of mobiles and stabiles
there, an ascending series of fragile mechanisms,
delicate metallic petals in perpetual activity
a pattern in silent metamorphosis, New York itself abstracted into art
the skyline above you is a shifting phantasmagoria,
slender and supple towers merging into bland acres of glass.
When we climbed into the skyline for the first time,
and looked out from the top of the Time-Life Building
the tops of the surrounding buildings were hidden in the clouds,
they could have been infinitely tall.
in the misty network below, neon signs were like tiny tongues of flame
licking the city's feet, Nothing was human, but the cabs were yellow confetti.

Anything can happen. I spent a day tracking down a Cummings play
published in 1927: went into every bookstore on 4th. Avenue,
and every owner had heard of it, had sold a copy six months ago,
advised me to go to the next store. One of them had his door locked,
opened it for us with a smile, then locked it behind us as we left.
Finally it was suggested that I ring the publisher,
who was supposed to have gone out of business many years ago.
I rang the number, and a voice said:
"Sure we got the book, come up to the 31st floor, 386 Fourth Avenue
and I'll sell you a copy"
and I went up in a silver bus, and a clanking elevator,
and there was a woman looking exactly like an aunt
with knitting and tea-cup and there was the book
three dollars ninety and a warm smile.

I have been in the city three times and maybe spent 100 hours
of my life there. These have included intense moments in the experience
of what we are pleased to call culture –
Chagall in the Museum of Modern Art,
the Moscow Art Theatre's Chekov –
But these are moments which live outside their ambience.
The city rather lives within me as Sunday morning
cheesecake in the automat, a burlesque show with jokes which Aristop-
hanes must have known, where the ancient comic grabbed the second
banana's waist-band, looked in and rasped:
"Hey there Jolly Green Giant, so what's new besides Ho HO Ho?"
the surrealistic landscape of flyovers and underpasses and
four lane freeways and triple decked bridges approaching Mannahattan,
the restless snarl of the police sirens as you lie in a hotel bed,
the astonishing hauteur of the majestic women
cruising in their cadillacs down a hysterical Fifth Avenue
as if it were the easiest thing in the world
instead of the most terrifying,
the little open skating rink a stone's throw from Saks;
if the whore had stopped for an answer I would have said yes I like it
but I could never live in it. Not that it's interested.

Poetry and Autumn

I saw a poem once; an old man brushing
Sun into heaps, with leaves in his hair.

And that September morning the trees were thrushing
Like mad; all the ingredients were there.

So words coughed awkwardly in the dry-cleaned air
Into shapes; and stood pathetically shivering.

I laughed with the old man, and we looked at where
The leaves in his layers of sun were singing.

Holiday Reading

Where did the Summer go?
In early May
I saw her coming down every street,
Her mouth wide with warm promises,
Coming with her ample apron full of
Buddha and St. John of the Cross and Freud and Plato
and other great replies
to the mysterious question sprung from
between her thighs.

Somehow she has evaded me.
There's no time now to explore.
The windows are growing rancid with frost,
The sky is all black drapery.
There's a white maggot of snow
Curled round the door.

Childhood

In my garden there hangs a tree upwards from the ground,
  A small tree, smaller than a man.
    What was it made my child's hands
      Fondle its thin body? (for I found
        And set it in grass)
          I do not know, except that now
I pluck its dead claws, and watch down
  On its crowded palms. It can no longer own
    Me, standing beside me in the barren soil.

Ulster Sequence: Parker's Fitts

1.
Here's the bus now. All aboard please.
Sore eyes in the convalescent
sun (good morning all) sliding
into the tundra between smiles.
The future is a kind of wide
arid silence, isn't it, ghostlit
neither by moon sun nor neon.
You gaze into it through the window
grime, like stout Cortez, laden
with heavy invisible luggage, yawn.
Travelling on Rapid Sic Transit.

2.
Thomas woke up with an oul and broken
refrain rattling in his head.
All night it'd nagged him round the bed –
the few black stumps of teeth twinging,
the mouth puckered with drawstrings
of old age and hangover parch –
all Erceldoune belling in Maytime
beyond the casement, each bell's tongue
the cock of a youth crowing, and bright
clangour of sun and voices from the street.
Thomas hawked up phlegm,
grunted at the creak in his knees,
the refrain banging away still –
till the words of it began to form
and his withered heart chimed in. Thomas
the Rhymer shouldered through the throng
in the street, their loud flux of lust,
selfish eyes eating each other –
True Thomas caught the blood-red bus
for Huntley Banks and the Elf Queen.

3.
It's no country for young men.
The bloodman's at the door again.
Transfusions feeding the curdled veins
of a septic mother. The gutters gorged.
Us think with blood. The land bloodlet.
The honourable members represent
constituencies of blood. And yet
we're all in the one red bus, all
in the same familiar skull, good morning
all. Seated thigh by thigh
and all our faces held in check,
held tight, fares please,
and gums mumbling the right word
that never comes, ruminating
in our fists the sure caress
that's never offered. Lovely day.

4.
On television the hounds had tugged
a hare into wriggling stumps.
They tucked their little fingers round
the wishbone, splintered it, he won,
his wish was for some switch to end
the agonies of bone and muscle.
His animal seemed pacified
with the chicken leg and the new boots,
but winced a bit from time to time
at his ragged voice which worried and worried
that butcher's floor, that carnal slime
of the thighs and wrists of girls that should be
tightening round a chosen lover.

5.
She knifed the bread and the bomb erupted.
The bomb was in his coat. As soon
as he touched the buttonholes it burst.
The news announcer broke down
the iron surgeon lost control
of his voice, the streets appeared to moan.
For a while we were all our animals
lurching through a voiceless howl,
wet paws belabouring parched eyes.
How do we staunch the wound in these
streets that's never let heal?

6.
I need shrove. You're bad with the nerves.
All night I was drinking the gas of the darkness
drowning me, bruising my eyes on the darkness
blinding me. His mind's not right.
It's panacea Tuesday, give us something quick,
a tab or a hit or a bottle or smoke.
But I don't want any more of your psycho -
chemical anodynes, medicine man.
Shrieve me, shrieve me. I want touching.

7.
Can't move for figures of speech.
Can't breathe your own breath.
The phrases have you by the throat,
tongue stalled like as not,
respected poetry skull cosmetics,
mouths fetid and phosphorescent
biting out of the dirty air,
poet bite and pundit bite.
You walk out blunted and you
put on smiles for bandages and
you walk out, all your senses fixed
and make a pass, for advertisers,
and the days are just other traffic
muttering past all the time.
Murmuring into your stunted ear.

8.

At some point between lathering face
and putting away the rinsed blade,
digested notion of annihilation.
A quiet bomb sloughed its petals,
knowledge became nerve tips.
Drained the basin, dabbed the blood
on my chin, gazed at the eyes above the towel.
Nothing new in them, nor any
badge to be worn saying, No Exit,
downtown Passchendaele, uptown Gomorrah.
No guilt to atone, no new wilderness
outside the bathroom, just the same old one
to wander in. There was a new nucleus
to it all, that's all. And words were all
pieces of a tumescent elegy.

9.

Her hair was dyed bright mediocre.
Give us a marriage-on-the-rocks, she says,
at the bar of the Emotional Safari room.
Enter the Emperor Highly Salacious
in search of his rations, munching suggestive
biscuits. Mine's a double, he calls.
Tearing a duster was the way she laughed.
Cars prowling the slick streets.
Same again. You and your animal
gestures! Steering wheel in sheathed
hands. He lifted his hands, the brute,
he tore my mind across. Same again.
Shod foot trampling the brakes,
the wipers whimpering on
the glass, erasing the spidery veins
and ferns as they form, ferns as they form.

10.
This one's me on my wounded ego
trip. See the swollen head
covered with puncture marks? That's it,
that's the ego for you, it's making
my neck all stiff. No more self-
centred sweeties, the doctor says, and also
cut down on adjectives. Of course the scenery's
lovely, volcanoes and black jagged crags,
and big dark forests and the sea crashing
and everything. Still. Wish you were here.

11.
Here's another previous face.
Do you ever take pity on your own lost face?
A fragile convalescent face,
scarcely a vestige, pale spectral
flotsam afloat in the fluid gloaming.
There's a dark bird lurking in the shadows of the hedge
behind those wasted shoulders, in
the deeps of those fear-exhausted eyes.
But it's not that failing light that makes
my heart fail now. It's the frail sac
of my twentieth year. Cameras kill.

12.
Surgeon was washing his hands, water
dripping down from the limp fingers.
He spied me there, laughed so burly
and hairy-armed, he looked like my mother's
butcher on the corner. Smiling,
laid out raw in all my canker,
watched the anaesthetist's eyes swivelling
as he held the needle in the crook of my arm.

That was a long time ago
in the old world. They clothed the wound,
drained it of infection, turned me
out on to the fevered streets
halt but alive. But the city was changed
to the grounds of a sanatorium,
nurses drifting in white through the trees
occasional curtained ambulances
sliding by with unspeakable cargo.

13.
The ecstasy that entered me
was a jackdaw crashing down the chimney
into a locked silent room,
claws scrabbling the sedate pictures
and vases to smithereens, the bowl
of apples pecked into a mush.
Their first thought, coming in,
was thieves, until they saw the beak-
scrawl on the mirror, and then its crumpled
bag of feathers behind the sofa.
On the whitewashed walls you can see the flurry
still of its soiled demented wings.

14.

O feed that puss, me foot them bills,
bare as a flare, all the way home,
the crowd cowed, me waltzing through,
the policeboys fistless, the stale moon
nothing more than a prune we chewed
and spat into the sky. Lord,
we all inhabit one another,
as the sky habituates the city:
we've all been willed to one another
by lady void, we're all each other's
heirlooms. Dance yourself bald,
the way the wind jigs a tree,
rag through the town, there's no salve,
no being saved, except we bless
our angel wrestlers up every street
and down again. I love you.

15.
Will you look at yon poetry man.
Hey, fatstock. Hopalong.
Give us a snatch of your clownish song.
He wants to shimmy rings round you.
He wants the world to love him to death.
He thinks that he's the man in the street
and that's who the streets belong to. Ask him
what side he's on, he'll tell you
the people's side – that's all the sides.
He wonders whether the next split
gutbag might be his own, maybe.
He's frightened his word'll be stubbed out.
But he belly laughs. He's not wise.

16.
Paleface mirrored in the window grime,
how you practise to dissemble.
These preying eyes, this mouth mad
to eat the city, pull them your lover
face, show us your cavities and
smile and smile and be a villain.
You're a house buzzing with glory holes.
You're a badge of all you've kissed and told,
you're the lovely man, a cast of millions.
Try and pull us your death mask. Try and
ingratiate yourself with soil.

17.
A lady that was brisk and bold
came riding o'er the fernie brae
a firehaired woman, who gave him his red
letter day. She made him glory in
his sad dishabells, in his glad rags.
She cancelled all of his dead letters;
and all the next day his senses clothed
in her salvation garments; hands
gloved in her dark musk, mouth
tender with her mouth, tongue
poignant with her breath, the coat
of her body cleaving to him as
he walks the street in all his canker.

18.
Please come round tonight, she says.
Bestow me some of your benedictions.
Don't bereave me. Don't be late.
He came to be awarded trophies,
Her photograph all eyes and hair,
A ring, all of the red letters,
the scented candle, the caught breath,
that summer's songs all impregnated
with their touch and awed gesture.
What will he do with this prize fodder?
Store it away in his heart's larder.

19.

You've caught me unawares, I try to
hold you down in my muscles till
they ache like fragrant bruises, but
you well up, irresistibly
tender, till – imagine my
amazement when my whole skin
breaks out in blatant smiles!
It's happiness, a species of
delirium. You give me it.
Nine tenths of the world's people
are dying for the lack of it
in any given night. This has
gone far enough, but
I want to go on saying it.
I haven't even mentioned yet
the curious ways you hold your face.
The best I can pay it is lip service.

20.
She served me up my words in a tart
sauce, saying, eat this up,
it'll do you good. I drew up the chair
to my diet of worms and tried a polite
morsel of my fiasco. O
the verbose gristle turned my stomach.
Perfect food for thought, I said,
but she reappeared from her secret kitchen
bearing me sweet relief from a shapely
jug of the milk of humankindness.

24.
Caught in the shadows under the arch
He's grit lodged under a heavy eyelid.
The night's spoor got lost somewhere
in the dark. One had smiled across
as if she would take him in a breath;
another's talk had seemed like the genuine
swag – now it was head rubble,
and the only eye that he was getting
was from the plunderer on the billboard.
Across the beach there are coils of water
glistening moist as grave jewels.

Skiff of Pain

O listen nurse the pleasure-boat is hooting
In the harbour all its pennants stiff
Its ballroom flashing with eyes and knives
And heels and fishy mouths along its wide ways
A hot coal flaring on the dark night water

Easy be easy the land is coming near

O the sea's lip is all curling over me
The shrouds howling by my head
The sky's hand pinning my forehead
And I fear the growling and the fishy mouths
And the cold cargo pressing on the black night water

Easy be easy the land is over there